Up The Faraway Tree

Also by Enid Blyton

Enid Blyton

Up The Faraway Tree

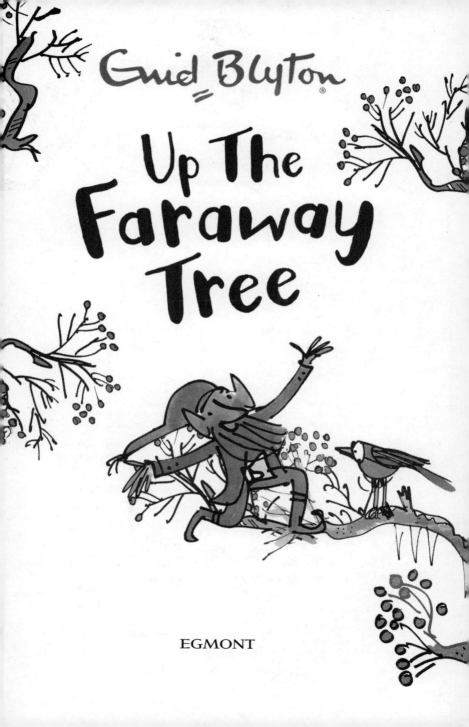

EGMONT

EGMONT

We bring stories to life

First published in Great Britain 1951 by Newnes
This edition published 2014
by Egmont UK Limited
The Yellow Building, 1 Nicholas Road, London W11 4AN

ENID BLYTON ® Copyright © 1951 Hodder & Stoughton Ltd

ISBN 978 1 4052 7224 7

3 5 7 9 10 8 6 4

www.egmont.co.uk

A CIP catalogue record for this title is available from the British Library

57711/4

Printed and bound in Great Britain by the CPI Group

MIX
Paper
FSC FSC® C018306

Contents

Off to the Enchanted Wood!

Once there were two children called Robin and Joy, and they read about the Faraway Tree in *The Enchanted Wood*.

'Let's go and find Joe, Beth and Frannie, the children who live near the Wood!' cried Robin. 'We'll ask them to take us there.'

Soon they came to the cottage where Joe and the girls lived. How pleased they were to see them!

'Come along,' said Joe. 'We'll take you to the Enchanted Wood and show you the Faraway Tree.' So off they went.

They came to the Enchanted Wood. It was dark and mysterious. 'Jump over this ditch,' said Joe. 'We follow that path.'

Down the winding path they went to the middle of the Wood – and there they saw a most extraordinary tree.

It was very, very big. 'It reaches to the clouds,' said Joe.
'And look – lots of people walk up and down the tree.'

'I want to climb it!' said Joy. 'Do let's. I've always
wanted to go up the Faraway Tree.' So Joe helped her
up.

It was a very peculiar tree. 'Look – there are oranges growing here,' said Joy, and she picked one.

But a little further up there were apples and pears! How very strange! Then suddenly Joy cried out with pleasure.

'Look! There's a little window in the tree. I *must* peep in.' And then what a shock she got!

The Angry Pixie lived there, and he didn't like people peeping at him. He threw a jug of milk all over Robin and Joy.

Joe wiped their clothes clean. 'The Angry Pixie always does that,' he said. 'Never mind. You can peep in at the next window all right.'

So they did – and they saw the Owl asleep with his red night-cap on. 'Doesn't he look sweet?' said Beth.

Little folk passed them up and down the tree. There were brownies, pixies, fairies, witches, and even rabbits and squirrels!

'This is a most exciting tree,' said Joy. 'Oh – whatever is that slishy-sloshy noise – look – there's water coming down the tree!'

Sure enough, a cascade of soapy water came pouring down the tree. Robin got soaked, but Joy hid under a branch.

'It's Dame Washalot's dirty water,' said Joe. 'Look, there she is, washing up there in her tub on that branch.'

And there she was! She waved to the children. 'Did my soapy water catch you? So sorry. I didn't know you were there.'

Dame Washalot had put her clothes to dry on a branch, and baby squirrels were sitting on them to keep them safe. How lovely!

'Look – here's a little yellow door,' said Joy. 'Who lives there?' 'Knock and see,' said Joe.

So Joy knocked – and the door flew open, and there stood little Silky the pixie, her golden hair in a cloud round her face.

'Hallo!' she said. 'Are these friends of yours, Joe? How nice! Let's go up and see old Moon-Face. Come along.'

So up the tree they went – and suddenly they saw someone sitting in a deck-chair, fast asleep, with his mouth wide open!

'That's Mister Watzisname,' said Joe. 'Oh,' said Robin,
'I *must* drop this plum into his mouth!'

Wasn't he naughty? He dropped the plum in before Joe
could stop him, and Watzisname swallowed it whole!

He woke up and began to choke. Joe had to bang him so hard on the back that his deck-chair fell down the tree.

A loud roar came up. 'Who's throwing chairs at me? I'll come up and get you!'

Up came a most peculiar man. He wore a saucepan for a hat, and was hung all round with jangling pans and kettles.

'It's the old Saucepan Man!' cried Joy, and she hugged him. 'I've always wanted to meet you, Saucepan!'

Saucepan forgot about the chair that had hit him. He beamed all round. 'Let's go and see Moon-Face and have tea,' he said.

So up they went to Moon-Face's door at the top of the tree. It opened – and there stood dear old Moon-Face!

'Come in!' said Moon-Face. 'You're just in time! I've got some Toffee Shocks I've made.' He led them into his room.

It was quite round. The furniture stood neatly round the inside of the tree-trunk. Moon-Face brought out the tin of Toffee Shocks.

'What's that hole in the middle of the room?' asked Robin, peering down it. 'Where does it go?'

'It goes to …' began Joe, and then he laughed. 'Look at Joy! Her Toffee Shock has got enormous – now it's burst – and Joy's so surprised!'

Moon-Face took them to the branch outside his room.
He pointed to where a yellow ladder led up through a
hole in the clouds.

'See that!' he said. 'That leads to whatever Land is at
the top of the Tree today. Like to go?'

'What Land is it?' asked Joy. 'The Land of Smacks,' said Moon-Face, so nobody wanted to go. 'Have a cushion?' said Moon-Face.

'You can slide down my hole from the top of the tree to the bottom on my cushions, if you like. Here's one for you, Joe.'

Soon they were all whizzing down the exciting Slippery-Slip inside the tree – round and round, and down and down!

Joy shot out through a little door at the bottom of the tree, and landed neatly on a mossy cushion. 'Lovely!' she said.

Then all the others shot out too. A little squirrel ran up to collect the cushions and take them back to Moon-Face.

'Well, that was a most exciting afternoon,' said Robin and Joy. 'Come again next week,' said Joe. 'There'll be an exciting Land to see then – we'll visit it!'

The next week Robin and Joy went to visit Joe, Beth and Frannie again, and they all set off for the Faraway Tree.

They climbed up it, but they didn't peep at the Angry Pixie. They hid under a branch when Dame Washalot's water came down.

Silky was out. So was Moon-Face. What a pity! 'Never mind – we'll climb up the ladder and see what Land there is above the clouds,' said Joe.

He popped his head out of the cloud. 'Quick!' he cried. 'It's a very exciting-looking Land – with a most *enormous* castle in the middle!'

It was a very peculiar Land indeed. There were all kinds of castles in it, some tiny, some large, and some enormous.

Then the children discovered a strange thing – the castles were growing! 'Look at this tiny one!' cried Beth.

They watched it grow from a little castle to a big one with a door. 'Let's go inside,' said Robin.

So in they went – and the door shut with a bang! And then the castle began to walk off with them.

'Where is the castle going?' cried Joe. 'Stop, stop!' He tried to open the door but it wouldn't move.

All the windows were barred. Joe shouted through one to a little pixie. 'Go and tell Moon-Face what's happened!'

28

The castle went past all the other castles, and came to a deep forest. It went right into the middle of it.

'This castle must have been ordered by somebody or other,' said Joe. 'Oh, dear – I wonder who it belongs to!'

The little pixie to whom Joe had called raced off to the
Faraway Tree. Moon-Face was in. The pixie shouted
to him.

'All the children have gone off to the Land of Castles
and they're in a castle that has walked off!'

'Good gracious!' said Moon-Face, and he rushed up to the Land of Castles. 'Where's that castle gone to?' he roared.

'It's one ordered by the Enchanter Red-Cloak,' said the pixies there. 'It's gone to the Dark Forest to await him.'

Poor Moon-Face! He didn't want to go to the Dark Forest at all, but he set off at once. Soon he came to it.

The Enchanter Red-Cloak had already arrived, and with him was the Witch Flyaway. She left her broomstick outside.

Moon-Face hid and watched them go into the castle.
Then he ran out and took the broomstick.

'You may come in useful!' he said. 'Fly up to the
windows, broomstick, so that I can look in!'

What was happening to the five children? The
Enchanter and the Witch *were* astonished to see them!

'Look! Five servants for us already!' cried the Enchanter.
And he set them all to work cleaning the castle.

Joe went to him. 'Please let us go. We didn't know this castle was meant for you.' 'No. You're prisoners!' said Red-Cloak.

But who is that peering in at the window? It is Moon-Face on the broomstick! He tapped on the window.

Joe saw Moon-Face and ran to the window. 'Oh, Moon-Face. You've come to rescue us – but the windows are barred!'

'The topmost ones aren't,' said Moon-Face. 'Go up to the top rooms. Quick, before the Enchanter comes back!'

The five children ran up the stone stairs, up and up and up – and a roar came after them. 'Where are you going?'

'Quick! The Enchanter and the Witch are coming!' panted Joe. 'Ah – here's a room without bars to the window!'

Moon-Face sailed in at the window on the Witch's broomstick. How glad they all were to see him!

'Get on the broomstick!' he cried. 'There's just room! Hurry, hurry! I can hear footsteps outside the door!'

They all got on just as the Enchanter and the Witch ran through the door. 'Our servants are escaping!' they cried.

But they couldn't stop them! The broomstick sailed out of the window, and went safely back to the Faraway Tree.

The Land of Roundabouts and Swings

After the adventure in the Land of Castles, Moon-Face said the children weren't to explore without him.

'Well, come with us tomorrow and we'll see what Land is there,' said Joe. 'It's the Land of Roundabouts and Swings,' said Moon-Face.

So next day they went up through the hole in the cloud – and there was the Land of Roundabouts and Swings!

'I'll ride on this elephant!' cried Joe. The others chose animals to ride on – and off went the roundabout!

But, dear me, when the roundabouts stopped, what do you think happened? All the roundabout animals walked off with their riders!

Joe went off on his elephant. Beth and Frannie were on giraffes. Robin was on a cat and Moon-Face on a dog.

But poor Joy was on a duck, and it rose into the air and flew away. 'Hey, come back!' cried Moon-Face.

The roundabout animals rushed about madly and the children couldn't get off. 'What's going to happen?' cried Joe.

'We've lost poor Joy,' said Robin, upset. 'Goodness
knows where her big white duck has gone with her.'

Just then the roundabout started off again, and, dear
me, as soon as the animals heard the music …

. . . They all rushed back to their places – and round and round they went as usual.

And what a good thing – Joy's duck came flying back, too, so everything was quite all right again.

'Now let's go on the swings,' said Moon-Face. 'They do go so nice and high. Come with me in my boat-swing, Frannie.'

The swings went very high indeed with the children – higher and higher, and higher . . .

And suddenly Moon-Face's swing swung right off its chains and went up into the air.

Everyone else's did the same. 'Help! Help! Are we going to crash?' cried the children in fright.

The boat-swings flew through the air – and then began
to fall – down, down, down – oh, dear!

But there was no accident – because the swings were
boats, and landed gently on a nearby lake!

'Oh, goodness me!' said Joy. 'What frights we get in this Land! I'm going to get out of my boat before it sails off!'

'Quick! We must go home!' cried Moon-Face. 'This Land is leaving the top of the Faraway Tree! Run, all of you!'

One day the children went to see Moon-Face and Joy told him that her birthday was the very next day.

'Now isn't that lucky – the Land of Wishes comes to the tree tomorrow,' said Moon-Face. 'We'll all go for your birthday treat!'

So into the Land of Wishes they went. A birthday child could always wish twelve wishes there – and they would all come true.

It was a lovely Land, full of pixies, brownies, gnomes and fairies, all ready to grant a birthday child's wishes.

'Now,' said Joy, who was a very nice child, 'I'm going to give each of you a wish. Moon-Face, what do *you* wish for?'

'A tiny aeroplane to fly in,' said Moon-Face. So Joy wished – and, hey presto, a tiny aeroplane appeared!

Moon-Face got in – whooooosh! Up he went and circled over their heads. Oh, how lovely!

'You shall each have a turn,' said Moon-Face, generously. 'You first, Joy, because it's your birthday.' What fun they had!

'Your turn for a wish now, Silky,' said Joy. 'I'd like magic shoes that can leap like a goat,' said Silky. And there they were!

Silky put them on – and off she went, leaping all over the place. 'Lovely!' she said. 'Thank you, Joy.'

Joe wanted a tiny train he could drive himself – and it suddenly appeared. Joe drove it proudly.

Beth and Frannie wanted dolls that could talk and walk – and really, the dolls were sweet when they arrived!

'Now you, Robin,' said Joy, 'what do *you* want?' 'A puppy of my own, please,' said Robin – and it appeared at once.

'Oh, what a darling!' cried everyone. But, dear me, you should have seen the puppy chase the two dolls!

'Now I'll wish for the biggest balloons you've ever had!'
said Joy – and I just wish *you* could have seen them!

They were so big that when the puppy caught hold of a
string, he sailed up in the air with the balloon!

Then Joy wished for a birthday tea – just look at it!
They all sat down to enjoy it.

The birthday cake was magnificent. It had nine candles
burning on it, and 'A Happy Birthday, Joy' was written
all round it.

Soon it was time to pull crackers – and, will you believe it, the crackers ran up on little legs!

There were wonderful caps and hats inside – the children did look grand in them. Even the dolls had caps.

'You've had eight wishes, Joy,' said Joe. 'What will you wish for next? You must wish for presents for yourself, too.'

'Well – I would love a new frilly frock,' said Joy, 'and shoes to match – and, oh, how I would love a pair of wings!'

Well, of course, she had them at once – see her flying
up in the air like a fairy!

She flew out of sight. 'I hope she won't lose her way,'
said Joe. 'I say – I believe this Land is moving on. Come
back, Joy!'

But Joy didn't come back. She was having a perfectly lovely fly by herself. She didn't know that the Land was going!

The children didn't like to go back to the Faraway Tree without Joy. Oh, dear – would they have to stay there always?

Then Joy came back – but the Land had left the Faraway Tree and the ladder to it was gone!

'I've one wish left!' cried Joy, remembering. 'I wish us all back safely in Moon-Face's room!' And, hey presto, there they were!

One day Moon-Face and the others were with the old Saucepan Man at the top of the tree.

And when Moon-Face made a joke the Saucepan Man laughed so much that he fell off the branch.

And when the others climbed down to find him, they saw a dreadful thing.

Poor old Saucepan had got his feet jammed into a big kettle – and he couldn't get them out!

'We shall have to take him to the Land of Magic when it comes, and get a spell to free his feet,' said Silky.

So poor Saucepan had to get along by leaping about in the kettle – he looked most peculiar!

When Dame Washalot saw him, she fled in fright and upset such a lot of hot water ...

. . . that she almost drowned poor Mister Watzisname sitting asleep on a branch below. He *was* cross!

At last the Land of Magic came to the top of the Tree.
The others helped Saucepan up the ladder.

The Land of Magic was very strange. There were all
kinds of pops and bangs and mists and fireworks!

'It's all the magic that's being made,' said Moon-Face.
'Look out – there's a whole heap of witch-cats coming!'

They got out of the way of the cats, who were all going
to belong to witches. But Saucepan fell over them!

'Keep out of any magic ring you see,' said Silky. 'If you are drawn in, goodness knows what might happen!'

Robin nearly got into one that he didn't see. He had half changed into a black cat when Joe pulled him back!

'It's awful to leap along with my feet in this kettle,' said Saucepan. 'There – I've leapt into a puddle!'

It was a magic puddle! Saucepan turned bright blue, and his ears grew a yard long! He did look odd.

'Oh, dear – this Land of Magic is quite dangerous,' said Silky. 'Hi, pixie – tell us where to buy spells.'

'At that Spell Shop,' said the pixie. 'Over there.' So they all went to the Spell Shop.

'A spell to change Saucepan to his right colour, please,'
said Joe, and was handed a yellow bottle.

'And a spell to get his feet out of this kettle,' said Beth,
and got a box of powder. Now to make the magic work!

The children poured the bottle over Saucepan – and there was a loud explosion! Everyone fell flat!

Saucepan disappeared. 'Oh, dear – was that the right magic?' said Silky. 'Saucepan, where are you?'

He suddenly appeared again, beaming. 'I'm pink now,' he said. 'Not bright blue. Isn't that good?'

Then they powdered his feet in the kettle – and they grew small so that he could get them out. How clever!

The Quarrellers

One day Moon-Face was giving a little tea-party on the branch outside his home ...

... when there was a loud noise from above, and down the ladder through the cloud came a crowd of shouting folk.

'Quick – into my house!' cried Moon-Face. 'The Land of Quarrels has come to the tree – and these are the Quarrellers!'

The Quarrellers banged on Moon-Face's shut door. 'Let us in! We want to take you back to our Land!'

'They'll break the door down!' cried Moon-Face, in despair. 'Quick, get cushions – we'll all slide down the Slippery-Slip!'

So one by one they slid down the Slippery-Slip at top speed ... and Moon-Face left as just as his door was broken in!

They shot out at the bottom of the tree one by one, and landed on the mossy turf. The squirrel collected the cushions.

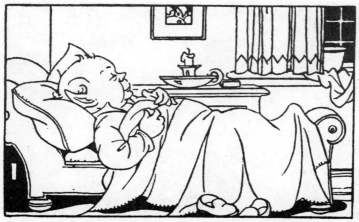

'Poor Moon-Face,' said Joe. 'Come home with us for the night – you shall sleep on our sofa.' So Moon-Face did.

Next day the tree was full of Quarrellers looking for
people to take back to their Land. All the little Tree-
Folk fled.

Then Moon-Face had a fine idea. 'I'll send a message to
the bees,' he said. 'They'll soon chase the Quarrellers
away.'

The bees were pleased. 'People who quarrel ought to be stung,' they said. 'We'll sting them!' And off they flew.

You should have seen the Quarrellers trying to get up the ladder as fast as they could! Nobody ever saw them again.

Here Comes Toyland!

Once, when everyone was having tea with Silky in her little house, the two dolls sat outside by themselves.

And a toy cat came down the tree and spoke to them. 'Hey, dolls! Toyland is at the top of the tree!'

'We'll come and visit it!' said the dolls, joyfully. 'It's our Land.' So up the tree they went.

And at the top was Toyland, with teddies and dolls and toy animals of all kinds – lovely!

The dolls didn't notice when the Land left the top of the tree and moved on. They cried when they knew.

'We want our mothers, Beth and Frannie!' they wept. So they sent a letter by the brownie postman.

It was delivered just as the children were leaving for Silky's tea-party. 'Listen to this!' cried Beth.

'Our dolls are in Toyland – and it's moved on from the tree. Whatever shall we do? Moon-Face, think hard!'

'I know!' cried Moon-Face. 'What about going off to fetch them from Toyland in my little aeroplane!' He got it out.

Off he went, waving goodbye. It was quite a long way to fly, but he got to Toyland at last. Where were the dolls?

There they were. They rushed madly to Moon-Face, and climbed into the aeroplane beside him. Off they went.

And how glad Beth and Frannie were to see them. 'You must never go away by yourselves again,' said Beth.

The Land of Cakes

Moon-Face was excited next day. 'Do you know, the Land of Cakes is at the top of the tree today?' he said.

'We'll go and collect a whole lot and give a grand Tree-Party. Come along!' So up to the Land of Cakes they went.

Oh, the cakes there! Chocolate and ginger, cream and fruit, cherry and every kind you could think of!

Look at that collection they brought back with them! 'Now to send out the invitations by the squirrel,' said Joe.

Well, everyone came to the party. Saucepan came with a brand new bow round his neck, beaming at everyone.

Dame Washalot came and Mister Watzisname. All the little squirrels came, and the owl and the Angry Pixie.

The cakes were delicious. It was a pity the cream one
fell on the Angry Pixie's head, but he was quite nice
about it.

We'll leave them there, enjoying their tea. Goodbye
for a while, little Tree-Folk. Wave to us – that's right.
Goodbye!

And now for a special Faraway Tree adventure!

Illustrations by Jan McCafferty

Up to the Land of Toys

KNOCKITY-KNOCK-KNOCK!

Bang-bang-BANG!

Rat-a-tarra-TAT!

'Good gracious! It sounds as if somebody's at the door!' said Joe. 'I'll go and open it, Mother.'

He went to open the door – and outside, looking very impatient, stood the Old Saucepan Man. He was hung about with pots and pans and kettles as usual, and had a saucepan for a hat.

'Hello,' said the Saucepan Man, 'didn't you hear me knock? I've come to tell you that we must go to the top of the Faraway Tree tomorrow. There's a very nice land coming there.'

'What is it?' asked Joe.

'Toyland,' said Saucepan. 'You could bring a bag with you and collect quite a lot in time for Christmas.'

'Oh what a good idea!' said Joe. He called to his two sisters. 'Beth! Frannie! Did you hear what the Saucepan Man said?'

'Yes!' they cried running to the door. 'Oh, Saucepan, we really must come. Can we help ourselves to toys, do you think?'

'Well, I've an aunt there,' said Saucepan, 'and if I tell her you're my friends, you can have what you want. Can you meet me at the top of the Faraway Tree tomorrow morning?'

'Oh, yes – and will Moon-Face and Silky be coming too?' asked Beth, happily. 'We haven't seen them for ages.'

'We'll have *fun*!' said Frannie.

'Yes, please,' said Saucepan unexpectedly. 'I'd like one very much.'

'Like what?' said Beth, astonished.

'What you just offered me – a bun,' said Saucepan, looking round for it.

'Oh – you suddenly went deaf,' said Beth. 'I just said – we'll have FUN.'

'Oh! All the same I'd like a bun,' said Saucepan.

Joe got him a bun out of the cake-tin. He went off, munching happily, his pans rattling and clanging round him. 'See you tomorrow!' he called.

The next day the three children set off to the Faraway Tree. Into the dark Enchanted Wood they went, and followed the winding path they knew so well. The trees whispered round them as they went. They always seemed to have secrets to tell one another. 'Wisha-wisha-wisha,' they whispered.

They came to the Faraway Tree in the middle of the wood. It looked even more enormous than usual. It towered up into the clouds, and the children couldn't

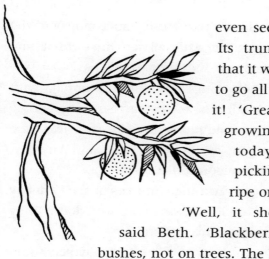

even see the top of it. Its trunk was so big that it was quite a walk to go all the way round it! 'Great! The tree's growing blackberries today,' said Joe, picking some big ripe ones.

'Well, it shouldn't then,' said Beth. 'Blackberries grow on bushes, not on trees. The Faraway Tree's made a mistake!'

They began to climb the tree. A little way up it stopped growing blackberries and grew pine-cones!

'Not so good,' said Joe. 'We can't eat pine-cones, Faraway Tree.'

'It's a very *exciting* tree, this,' said Frannie. 'Always growing different things all the way up – and having people living in it too – and a slippery-slip all the way inside from the top to the bottom. I'm glad we live near a tree like this. We're lucky.'

'Yes. I bet a lot of children wish they lived near it too,' said Joe, helping Beth over a steep bit. 'My goodness, the adventures we've had!'

'Look out – I can hear Dame Washalot's dirty water coming down!' yelled Frannie suddenly.

And, sure enough, down came a cascade of soapy

water, running down the trunk, splashing on the boughs, and soaking a little pixie who was sitting nearby.

'Bother!' she said. 'And I brought an umbrella with me, too, in case I didn't hear the water coming!'

Joe laughed. 'I should put on a swim-suit next time and not bother about an umbrella,' he said. 'Anyway, the sun will soon dry you!'

They went up, passing little windows in the Faraway Tree, and came to Silky's small yellow door. They knocked, but there was no answer.

'She's gone up to the top of the tree, I expect,' said Joe. 'Come on – we don't want to keep the others waiting.'

They climbed right up to Moon-Face's little door. From inside came the sound of chattering, and the noise of jangling and clanging.

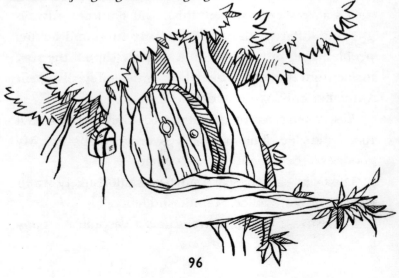

96

'The Saucepan Man's there all right,' said Joe. 'And the others, too, I should think.' He banged on the door. Moon-Face opened it, beaming all over his big round face. 'Oh, come in,' he said. 'We're just having a snack before we go.'

'What sort of snack?' asked Beth, going in with the others. 'Pop cakes? I love those.'

'No – something Saucepan bought when he was in the Land of Surprises,' said Moon-Face. 'Well-I-Never Rolls.'

'What a peculiar name,' said Joe, looking at the dish of nice crusty little rolls. 'What do they taste of?'

'Try one,' said Moon-Face. 'And tell us!'

Joe took a roll and bit into it. 'Tastes of cheese,' he said. 'No – well I never, it tastes of ginger now. No, it doesn't – it's chocolate! And now it tastes of coconut – and it's got bits of coconut in it – no, they've gone – it's treacly now. Well I never!'

'Yes. Most peculiar, isn't it?' said Moon-Face. 'No wonder they're called Well-I-Never Rolls. You just simply never know what they'll taste of next. Every chew you have tastes of something different.'

'Jolly good,' said Joe. 'I'll have another. My – this tastes of pickled onions – no, it doesn't – it's custard – lovely!'

'Mustard,' said Saucepan in disgust. 'I'd hate one to taste of mustard.'

'I said CUSTARD,' said Joe, and then made a face.

'Oh my goodness, it *is* mustard now. Horrible!'

'Just what I said. Mustard,' said Saucepan. He bit into his. 'Ah – mint! Delicious! Why, it's mint sauce, I can taste the tiny bits of mint.'

'You'll find you've got roast lamb next,' said Silky.

Saucepan looked surprised. 'No – it isn't ham,' he said.

'I said LAMB!' shouted Silky.

'No, it's not jam,' said Saucepan. 'Well I never, it's lamb! Lamb and mint sauce – how clever! Really these rolls are remarkable.'

So they were. The six of them finished up the whole dish of them. 'I wish I'd brought heaps more,' said Saucepan, getting up. 'Well, aren't we going up to Toyland? Do hurry up.'

They were all ready. They went out of Moon-Face's little round room and climbed up the topmost branch into a cloud. They came to the little ladder that led upwards through the last bit of cloud. Toyland should be at the top!

Saucepan went first. He climbed off the top rung of the ladder, and called down to the others.

'Yes, it's here. Come on!'

Up they all went, and at last stood in Toyland. But there seemed to be no toys about at all. Saucepan pointed to a town not far off. Flags were flying brightly from little houses.

'There's the Village of Toys,' he said. 'Now we'll go

and find my aunt.'

They set off to the village. But when they got there, Saucepan stopped and looked puzzled.

'Dear me,' he said, 'this isn't the land I hoped. The toys are all alive – look, isn't that a teddy bear walking about?'

'Yes,' said Beth. 'Goodness – we can't take toys like these away to play with at home! They're as big as we are!'

'I'll find my aunt,' said Saucepan, and they all walked down the village street, meeting three or four sailor dolls, a curious man who had no legs but just wobbled along, and some beautifully dressed dolls.

Saucepan's aunt was nowhere to be found. She kept a toyshop, and, of course, there was no toyshop there, because the toys lived in little houses made of coloured wooden bricks.

'Your aunt lives in the other land, you silly,' said Silky. 'This must be the Land of Toys, not Toyland.'

'Oh, well – let's enjoy ourselves, anyway,' said Saucepan. 'Here comes another wobbly man. Let's try and push him over.'

The wobbly man was astonished and annoyed when Saucepan gave him a push. He wobbled over backwards and then came forwards again, only to get another push, this time from Moon-Face.

'How dare you?' cried the wobbly man in a rage. 'That's not the way for visitors to behave! I'll report you

to the Captain of the Toy Soldiers!'

He wobbled off at a remarkable speed. The three children and Silky felt a bit scared.

'You shouldn't go round pushing people, Saucepan,' said Joe. 'Not even to see them wobble. I do hope we don't get into trouble.'

Saucepan suddenly went deaf and didn't hear. He hardly ever did hear when somebody scolded him. 'Look, there's a clockwork mouse running along!' he said, pointing. 'Run, mouse, run! Meeow! MEEOW!'

The clockwork mouse was very frightened when it heard Saucepan mewing. It turned and ran off at top speed, almost bumping into a toy soldier.

'Look – there's the Captain of the Soldiers,' said Beth, afraid. 'And the Wobbly Man is with him. He's complained about us, as he said he would. We'd better run away.'

'No,' said Joe. 'We can easily explain, and Saucepan must say he's sorry.'

Up marched the toy soldier, as smart as could be. He saluted – click!

'You must come with me,' said the Captain, in a commanding voice. 'You are not toys, and should not be here. Also, your behaviour must be looked into. Follow me, quick MARCH!'

'We'd better follow,' said Joe. 'He can't do anything to us; he's only a toy, even if he *is* alive. And I must say I'd rather like to see what that toy fort is like inside.'

So they all followed the toy soldier and the wobbly man. Whatever was going to happen?

They get into trouble

The Captain took them through the village and up to the wooden fort. It was very like a toy fort that Joe had once had. It even had a wooden drawbridge that could be pulled up or let down.

It was let down for them to walk over. Toy cannons stood here and there. Joe went up to one. 'Funny old cannon!' he said. 'Look, there's a knob to pull back and then let go, just like the toy cannon I had in my little fort at home.'

He pulled back the knob, let it go and then BANG! The cannon went off with a loud noise! The wobbly man was so shocked that he almost fell over, and it took a lot of wobbles for him to stand upright again.

The toys in the village below were so frightened when the cannon went BANG that they rushed out of their little houses and ran for their lives! The Captain was very angry indeed.

'Now see what you've done!' he said to Joe. 'Let off the cannon, and scared everybody! You must be mad.'

'I'm very sorry,' said Joe. 'I never thought the cannon would go off like that.'

'Well, what did you think it would do?' said the

Captain, angrily. 'Whistle a tune or dance a jig?'

Nobody dared to laugh. The Captain led them on again, and soon they came to a door that led into a wooden tower. They went in and found themselves in a room with a table and a chair at one end, and nothing else. The Captain sat himself down in the chair.

'Stand up straight,' he said. Everyone stood up very straight, even Saucepan.

'Salute,' said the Captain, and everyone saluted, though Moon-Face used the wrong hand.

'Dismiss!' said the Captain, and everyone stared. What did he mean?

'No – that's wrong,' said the Captain. 'Don't dismiss. Stand at ease.'

They obeyed. The Captain rapped loudly on the table. 'You are accused of not being toys. You are accused of punching wobbly men. You are accused of setting off cannons. You –'

'Only *one* wobbly man, and *one* cannon,' said Joe. 'We're sorry and we won't do it again. We'll dismiss now!'

But before they could go they heard the noise of marching feet, and into the room came about fifty toy soldiers, all very wooden. They surrounded the children and the others.

'To the deepest dungeon with them!' shouted the Captain.

'NO!' shouted Joe, and he pushed the nearest soldier

103

hard. The soldier fell against the soldier next to him and knocked him over. That one fell against the next one and he went down, too, knocking the soldier next to him – and before five seconds had passed every soldier was lying flat on the floor.

'It's like playing dominoes – knock the first over, and down goes the whole row!' said Frannie with a giggle.

The Captain looked alarmed. What was he to do with people like these? Goodness – one push, and all his soldiers were down! He banged on the table.

'Order! Order! Get up! Do you think you are skittles, men?'

The men got up, but none of them would go near the little group of six prisoners.

'Now listen,' said the Captain. 'Either you become toys, or you go to the deepest dungeon. You can choose.'

'All right – we'll be toys, then!' said Joe with a grin. 'I'll be a clockwork clown, and go head-over-heels all the time!'

He began to go head-over-heels all round the room, and knocked into one of the soldiers. Down they all went again, like a row of skittles!

'Right – you're a clockwork clown,' said the Captain. 'What will *you* be?' and he pointed at Moon-Face.

'A teddy bear,' grinned Moon-Face, 'with a growl in my middle.' And he pressed himself in the middle and pretended to growl.

'I'll be a doll,' said Silky, and began to walk about stiffly like a doll.

'And I'll be a furry grey rabbit!' said the Saucepan Man. 'I'll grow long floppy ears and grey fur!'

'We'll be dolls,' said Beth and Frannie together, and they walked about stiffly like Silky, giggling all the time.

'Right,' said the Captain thankfully. 'You are now toys, and can remain in the Land of Toys. Dis-MISS!'

The six of them went out laughing, Joe still turning head-over-heels, just for fun. They went over the drawbridge and into the town. In the distance they saw an enormous Noah's Ark.

'Let's go and see the animals coming out two by two,' said Beth, and they set off.

Frannie was just going to say something to Saucepan, who was in front of her, when she stopped. She stared hard.

She saw something very peculiar. Saucepan wore a saucepan for a hat, as usual – but, goodness, he had suddenly grown two huge floppy ears! The saucepan sat on top, looking very odd.

'Saucepan,' said Frannie, astonished. 'Saucepan, what's wrong with you?'

Saucepan turned round, surprised, and everyone got a tremendous shock. His face was covered in grey fur and he had very long whiskers!

'He's a toy rabbit!' said Frannie, with a squeal.

'Saucepan – you're a toy rabbit! You said you would be, and now you are.'

They were all very surprised. They stared and stared at poor Saucepan. How peculiar to see his face all grey, topped with two floppy ears and long quivering whiskers!

Saucepan looked at himself in one of his bright pans, which he used as a mirror. He was shocked to see such a furry face looking back at him. He gazed round at the others, scared.

Then he gave a shout and pointed to Joe. 'Well! Look at *him*! He's a clockwork clown now, hat and all! Yes, and he's got a key in his back! Joe, you're a clown! No wonder you keep going head-over-heels!'

Joe turned another somersault at once. The others gazed at him. Yes, Joe was a clown, with a clown's hat and suit. His face was daubed in red and white like a clown's too.

Frannie looked at the others, and squealed again.

'Look at Moon-Face – he's a fat, round little teddy bear, with a round, teddy-bear face that's hardly like Moon-Face's at all! Oh, Moon-Face – is it really you?'

'Yes,' said Moon-Face, putting up his hand to feel his face. 'Oh dear – I've gone all furry. Where are my clothes? They've gone.'

Joe pressed him in the middle and an alarming growl came out – grrrrrrrrrr!

'Don't,' said Silky. 'You made me jump. Don't press

him again, Joe. Oh, my goodness –
this is dreadful. We're all toys. Look
at *me*!'

'You're not so bad,' said Joe, looking
at her. 'You are the prettiest doll I ever saw.
And Beth and Frannie are dolls, too. Look at them
walking about, as stiff as can be. Beth, can you sit
down?'

'Not very easily,' said Beth, trying to sit on a nearby
wall. 'I can't seem to bend. And I can't shut my eyes,
either.'

'Perhaps they will shut when you lie down,' said
Moon-Face, speaking in a funny growly voice.

So Beth lay down on some grass for a moment and
at once her eyes shut!

'Yes, we're *really* toys,' said Frannie. 'It must have

begun to happen when we said we'd be toys, and chose what we'd be. But we only said it for fun.'

'I know. But you never know what will happen in the lands that come to the top of the Faraway Tree,' said Joe. 'Moon-Face, will we stop being toys when we get out of this land?'

'No, I don't think so,' said the teddy bear. 'And anyway, how do you think you are going to head-over-heels down the Faraway Tree? We'll just have to hope this will all wear off.'

'I don't like being a toy rabbit,' said Saucepan sadly. 'I feel silly. Do you think my face will become my own again if I wash it?'

'No,' said Joe, turning head-over-heels for about the fiftieth time; 'toy rabbits always stay furry. It's your ears that look so funny with that saucepan stuck on top of them. Why don't you take it off?'

'Well, I might get a cold,' said Saucepan. 'I always wear a hat. I don't feel right without a saucepan for a hat.'

'You certainly don't *look* right now,' said Moon-Face, in his growly voice.

'Nor do you,' said Saucepan. 'I wish you'd look like Moon-Face again. I don't like you like that.'

'Oh, come on,' said Joe, going head-over-heels again. 'Let's explore the Village of Toys and hope all this wears off. If only I didn't have to go head-over-heels so often! I'm getting very tired of it.'

'So are we,' said Frannie, getting out of his way. 'Do keep over there, Joe – you'll knock me over.'

The little group went on through the Village of Toys. Nobody took much notice of them now because they looked exactly like toys. Wobbly men wobbled about, looking very busy, and teddy bears lazed around, fat and cheerful looking. Dolls of all kinds went here and there, and they saw the little clockwork mouse again.

'Meeow!' said Saucepan, and it fled.

'You're unkind to it,' said Frannie. 'It's a dear little thing. Oh, dear – I do feel funny, walking stiffly like this. I'm sure I couldn't run, even if I had to!'

'Look, here come the Noah's Ark animals,' said Joe, getting up from another somersault. 'Two by two, just as they should. Two lions, two bears, two rabbits . . .'

'Two ducks, two mice,' went on Frannie.

'MEEOW!' said Saucepan at once again. 'Meeow!'

But the Noah's Ark mice took no notice of him. However, somebody else did! Behind the mice were two cats, and one of them left the row of animals and came over to Saucepan, glaring at him.

'What did you say just then?' said the wooden cat.

'Meow,' said Saucepan, 'meow, meow, meow!'

'How dare you call me such rude names!' said the cat, and showed claws in her wooden paws. Saucepan backed away hurriedly.

'I didn't mean to call you names,' he said. 'I just said, "meow, meow, meow," to the mice.'

'Well, that means, "You're a very ugly cat with a crooked tail!"' said the cat angrily. 'My tail is *not* crooked. Don't use cat-language if you don't know what it means!'

'Get back into line, cat!' called Mr Noah, and the cat obeyed. Saucepan was very relieved. Goodness – to think those simple meows had meant all that in cat-language! He really must be careful.

'Let's go on,' he said to the others, who were as surprised as he was. 'Moon-Face might suddenly begin to growl, and goodness knows what that might mean in bear-language! We don't want those two white bears and the two brown ones to come after us.'

'Well, let's go another way,' said Joe, gloomily turning another somersault. 'Blow this head-over-heels business. I'm tired of it!'

They turned down another way. Oh, dear – was this strange spell wearing off yet? It didn't seem like it!

Mr Oom-Boom-Boom

They came to a little garage. A very furry rabbit was busy putting petrol into a car driven by another toy rabbit. They looked at Saucepan in surprise as he came along with the others.

'Hello!' said the garage rabbit. 'What's the idea of wearing a saucepan for a hat? I can't say I've ever seen a rabbit wearing a hat before.'

'Well, you've seen one now,' said Saucepan, not very politely. 'Bother these awful floppy ears. I hate them. They make me look like a toy rabbit.'

'Well, you *are* a toy rabbit, floppy ears and all,' said the rabbit, staring.

'That's where you're wrong,' said Saucepan. 'I'm not. I hate being one. Ugly creatures, with stupid long ears and quivering whiskers!'

'Stop it, Saucepan,' said Joe, in a warning voice. He turned to the surprised rabbit.

'You must excuse him,' he said, 'he's really a Saucepan Man, as you can see. And I'm not really a clockwork clown, I'm a boy. Oh – excuse me, I can feel another somersault coming on!'

He turned head-over-heels and then stood up

111

straight again.

'I see,' said the rabbit. 'Well, I should just hate to be an ugly little Saucepan Man, so I know what he feels about being a rabbit – though rabbits are very handsome creatures – like myself. He should be pleased he's turned into one.'

'Well, we really like being ourselves best,' said Frannie. 'I'm a little girl, not a doll. And this teddy bear is really Moon-Face.'

'Never heard of him,' said the rabbit. 'Didn't know there were such things as Moon-Faces.'

Frannie giggled. Silky went up to the rabbit and smiled at him. 'Please do help us,' she said.

The rabbit stared at her. He thought she was the prettiest doll he had ever seen in the Village of Toys. The rabbit who was inside the car leaned out.

'Of course we'll help you,' he said. 'What do you want us to do?'

'Well, we did hope all this would wear off,' said Silky in a high doll's voice that was quite sweet. 'But it hasn't. And we wondered if you knew how we could get back into ourselves again.'

The two rabbits looked at one another. 'Difficult,' said one. 'Very,' said the other.

'What about the old Spell-Maker, Mr Oom-Boom-Boom?' said the first one. 'If he's in a good mood, he might do something for them.'

'Yes. But if he's in a bad mood, he might turn them

into something worse,' said the second rabbit.

'Then we won't go there,' said Joe hurriedly, and turned another somersault.

'We could see if he's in a good or bad mood before we say anything,' said the rabbit. 'I'll take you there in my car, if you can all squeeze in.'

'Well, we could try,' said Moon-Face, his little round teddy-bear face looking worried.

The rabbit told Silky to sit next to him. He thought she was really beautiful, and very sweet. 'I am sure, if *you* went to ask Mr Oom-Boom-Boom a favour he would say "yes" at once,' he said. 'I never saw anyone as pretty as you.'

'Well you're a very handsome rabbit,' said Silky, and that pleased him very much. They all squeezed into the car somehow, waved to the friendly garage rabbit, and set off.

'I feel a somersault coming on,' said Joe suddenly. 'I'm so sorry – but will you please stop the car so that I can get out and turn head-over-heels?'

'You're going to be a bit of a nuisance,' said the rabbit driver. 'Can't you do about a dozen, and make those do for a while?'

'I'll try,' said poor Joe. So he got out and did nine, but no more would come, so he got back into the car. 'I do wish you didn't wear so many pans and kettles,' he said to Saucepan. 'Move that kettle, will you? It's sticking its spout into me.'

113

'Kettles don't have snouts,' said Saucepan.

'SPOUT, I said, not Snout,' said Joe crossly. 'Now there's something else sticking into me – a saucepan handle.'

'I haven't got any candles,' said Saucepan, mis-hearing again. 'You know I haven't. You're just making a fuss, with all your chatter about snouts and candles.'

'I said SHOUTS and PANDLES,' bawled Joe, losing his temper. 'No, I don't mean that – I mean, I mean...'

'Pouts and Scandles,' said Frannie with a squeal of laughter. 'Be quiet, you two. Saucepan, dear, be sensible. He meant Spouts and Handles – look, they're sticking into him.'

'Well, why didn't he say so then,' grumbled Saucepan, moving the kettle and the saucepan and sticking them into Moon-Face instead. 'Goodness, Moon-Face, what are *you* growling about now?'

Moon-Face turned his teddy-bear face to Saucepan. 'You're not kind,' he said.

'No, I don't mind,' said Saucepan, whose hearing had gone quite wrong with the noise of the car and the jangling of his pans. 'Of course I don't mind. Why should I mind? Mind what, anyhow?'

'Stop talking,' said the rabbit at the wheel. 'I keep listening and it all sounds so mad that I'm sure I shall drive into a tree or something. Anyway, I want to talk to this dear doll here, Silky.'

Nobody talked after that except Silky and the toy

rabbit. The car went on and on, and at last Joe wanted to get out and go head-over-heels again. 'Can you stop?' he called.

'Goodness, I've gone right past Mr Oom-Boom-Boom!' said the rabbit, putting on the brake so suddenly that the saucepan flew off Saucepan's head and rolled away down the road. 'Yes, get out and somersault for a bit while I turn the car round.'

So Joe turned about ten somersaults, while the toy rabbit turned the car round again. Then back they went to find Mr Oom-Boom-Boom.

'Don't start talking to Silky or you'll go right past again,' begged Frannie. But this time the rabbit kept an eye open for Mr Oom-Boom-Boom's house and suddenly put on the brakes again.

OOM BOOM BOOM
KNOCK
SEVEN TIMES

'There goes another of my saucepans,' groaned Saucepan. 'Do we have to stop so suddenly?'

Nobody took any notice of him. They stared at a funny little door set in a grassy hill. On it was printed in bold black letters:

OOM-BOOM-BOOM. KNOCK SEVEN TIMES.

'Silky, you go,' said Frannie. 'Perhaps Oom-Boom-Boom will be nice to you. You really do look very sweet.'

'All right. I'll knock,' said Silky bravely, though she felt very scared. She got out of the car, and went up to the little door. She took hold of the knocker and knocked seven times – blam-blam-blam-blam-blam-blam-blam!

A loud voice came from inside. 'Stop knocking. Once is quite enough!'

'Oh dear – he's in a bad mood!' called the rabbit. 'Come back quickly, Silky, and we'll drive off.'

'I can't come,' wailed Silky. 'The knocker has got hold of my hand. It won't let go!'

Joe jumped out at once and went to help her. But Silky was quite right. The knocker had tight hold of her hand and wouldn't let it go.

Moon-Face went to help, too, and then the Saucepan Man, looking very worried. And just at that very moment the door opened, pulling poor Silky with it, and a voice boomed out loudly:

'WHAT'S ALL THIS? DISTURBING ME IN THE

MIDDLE OF MY SPELLS!'

Everyone thought that Oom-Boom-Boom was a very good name for him, booming at them like that. But he wasn't a bit like his voice. He was an old pixie with a beard so long that it trailed behind him. He had big, pointed ears, and wore a funny little round hat with feelers on it like a butterfly's. His eyes were as green as grass and very bright indeed.

He frowned at them all – and then he saw Silky, still held by the knocker.

'Ah,' he said, and a smile broke over his face like the sun shining out suddenly. 'Ah! What a dear little doll! No wonder my knocker wouldn't let you go. Where did you come from? I've never seen a doll as pretty as you! Do you know where you ought to be?'

'No,' said Silky, with a gasp.

'You ought to be standing at the very top of the great big Christmas Tree that Santa Claus has in his castle!' said Oom-Boom-Boom in his booming voice. 'He's always looking for the prettiest doll in the world to put there, but he's never found one as pretty as you yet!'

'I'm not a doll,' said Silky. 'I'm a fairy. I've been turned into a doll today.'

'Let her go, knocker,' said the pixie. 'Come in, all of you. Why have you paid me this visit?'

'He seems in a very good mood now,' whispered Joe to Moon-Face. 'I think it's safe to go in.'

They all went in and the door shut with a bang that

made them jump. Inside there was a narrow, very winding passage that led into the hill. They followed the pixie down it, everybody stumbling over his very long beard that trailed out behind him. He didn't seem to mind.

He took them to a big room with a very low ceiling. A great fire burned in the middle, but the flames were green, not red, and no heat came from them.

'I was just making a few spells,' said Oom-Boom-Boom, his big voice echoing all round the room. 'I'm a spell-maker, you know.'

'Yes. That's why we came,' said Silky, feeling very nervous. 'Please, dear Mr Oom-Boom-Boom, will you use a spell to help us? We want to go back to our right selves. I'm a fairy, really, as I told you.'

'And we're really little girls,' said Beth and Frannie. 'And this clown is a boy, and the toy rabbit is Old Saucepan Man...'

'And I'm Moon-Face,' said Moon-Face, his little teddy-bear face looking very earnest. 'Please do help us.'

'Ha,' said Oom-Boom-Boom, looking round at them and beaming, 'well, I don't mind doing that. That's easy. But I'll do it on one condition.'

'What's that?' asked Joe, his heart sinking.

'I'll turn five of you back to your own shapes – but I want this little doll here, the very pretty one, to stay with me so that I can sell her to Santa Claus to put on the top of his Christmas Tree! It will be such an honour

118

for her. You'd love that, wouldn't you, my dear?' he said to Silky, turning to her.

Silky looked very frightened. 'Well – I'll stay and let you sell me to Santa Claus,' she said, 'if you will use a spell on the others.'

'Oh, dear, darling Silky!' said Moon-Face, putting his furry arm round her, 'How sweet you are! But we wouldn't let you. We'd never leave you here alone.'

'Never,' said Joe. 'NEVER!'

'Never, never, never, never,' said Joe, Beth and Frannie.

'I'm going to stay,' said Silky, looking as if she was going to cry, but smiling at them all the same. 'It won't be so bad, going to Santa Claus, though it sounds very dull standing on the top of his Christmas Tree. But it's for you, you see, so I want to do it!'

'Of course she wants to do it,' said Oom-Boom-Boom. 'She's a sensible little doll.'

'Be quiet,' said Joe. 'I tell you we won't let her do it! We'd rather be toys all our lives than that!'

Then Mr Oom-Boom-Boom lost his temper. He rushed at Joe – but Joe did a very clever thing. He caught him by his very long beard, dragged him to a big table and tied him to it with his beard, making dozens of knots!

'Now, quick, let's go!' he cried. 'Sorry about tying you up, Oom-Boom-Boom, but you're not going to have Silky. Run everyone!'

119

They ran up the winding passage and came out on the hillside. And oh, thank goodness, there was the rabbit waiting in his car! What a wonderful sight!

In Santa Claus's castle

Joe got to the car first. 'Quick!' he cried. 'I can hear Oom-Boom-Boom coming! He must have got free.'

So he had! He appeared at the door of his peculiar house, and they saw that he had freed himself by cutting his beard short. He did look strange.

The toy rabbit revved up his car and it shot off, almost before Saucepan was safely in. A kettle flew, clanging, down the road, and Saucepan groaned.

'Well, thank goodness that kettle's gone,' said Joe. 'It can't stick into me again. Oh, dear – I feel I want to turn head-over-heels.'

'Well, you can't,' said Moon-Face firmly. 'Unless you want to be caught by the Oom-Boom-Boom fellow. Here, Saucepan, hang on to Joe, and stop him turning head-over-heels in the car!'

It was difficult to stop him, but they managed it. After they had gone a good way the rabbit stopped the car for a talk, and Joe took the chance of turning about a dozen somersaults.

'You know, I think you should go to the Land of Santa Claus,' said the rabbit. 'I do really. Not to give him Silky, of course, that would never do – but to tell him you aren't toys and to ask him if he can stop you being what you're not.'

'That's a bit muddling,' said Moon-Face, trying to work it out. 'Yes – it seems a good idea. After all, he deals in toys, doesn't he? He must know them very well. He'll be able to tell we're not real toys, and *might* help us.'

'We know he's kind,' said Silky. 'He's so fond of children. Let's go to him. How can we get there, though? This land may stay at the top of the Faraway Tree for some time – and the Land of Santa Claus may not be the next one to arrive.'

'That's true enough,' said the rabbit. 'Actually the next land on the timetable is the Land of Squalls, which doesn't sound too good. But I'll tell you what I can do for you!'

'What?' asked Joe.

'I can drive you to the next station and put you on a train for the Land of Santa Claus,' said the toy rabbit. 'I happened to notice that some trains there do go to his land. What about it, friends?'

'A very good idea,' said everyone, and off they went. They came to a funny little station after a while, and they all got out.

'I wish you could stay in my land for ever, Silky doll,' said the rabbit to Silky. 'You really are the prettiest thing I ever saw. But there – you'd be unhappy and I couldn't bear that.'

'I'll write to you,' said Silky.

'Will you really?' said the rabbit. 'Do you know, I've never had a letter in my life! It *would* make me feel important! Look, there's a train in!'

'Wow! This train's going to the Land of Santa Claus! What a bit of luck!' cried Moon-Face. 'Goodbye, rabbit. You really have been a good friend. I'll write to you.'

'My goodness – fancy me getting two letters!' said the delighted rabbit.

'We'll *all* write,' said Joe, shaking his furry hand warmly. 'Goodbye. It's been lovely meeting you.'

Silky gave him a kiss and he nearly cried for joy. 'I've never been kissed before,' he said. 'Never. A kiss – and letters – my goodness, I am a lucky rabbit!'

They all climbed into the train and waved goodbye.

'Nice fellow, that rabbit,' said Joe. 'Well, we're off again. I wonder how far it is.'

It was quite a long way, and they all fell asleep. A porter woke them up at last. 'Hey, you! Don't you want to get out here?' he said. 'This is where toys usually get out.'

They scrambled out because the station board said, 'Get out here for the Castle of Santa Claus!'

'Just in time,' said Joe, yawning. 'Oh – here I go, turning head-over-heels again!'

'There's the castle – look!' said Beth, pointing to a magnificent castle with many towers, rising high on a hill nearby. 'And, goodness – look at the snow! Anyone would think it was winter here.'

'Oh, it always is,' said the porter. 'It wouldn't be much good for sleighs, would it, if there wasn't snow? Is Santa Clause expecting you? His sleigh usually meets the train in case there are any visitors for him.'

'Is that it down there?' asked Moon-Face, pointing down into the snowy station yard. A sleigh was there, with four lovely reindeer, whose bells jingled as they moved restlessly. A small red pixie held the reins.

'Yes, that's the sleigh. Better go and get in,' said the porter. He stared hard at Silky. 'Goodness, isn't that a pretty doll? I bet Santa Claus will want her for his own Christmas Tree.'

They went to the sleigh and got into it. 'To Santa Claus, please,' said Joe, and off they went, gliding smoothly over the snow, drawn by the four eager reindeer.

They arrived at the castle. They felt rather nervous when they saw how big and grand it was. They stood at an enormous door, carved with all kinds of toys, and rang a great bell.

The door swung open. 'Please come in,' said a teddy bear, dressed like a footman. 'Santa Claus will see you in a few minutes.'

They went into a big hall and then into a great room, where many little pixies and goblins were at work. 'You might like to look round while you're waiting,' said the bear footman. 'You'll see the pixies painting the dolls' houses, and the goblins putting growls into us bears, and you'll see how the somersaults are put into the clockwork clowns.'

'I don't want to see that,' said Joe, feeling at once that he wanted to go head-over-heels. He turned a few and then stood up again. 'What are those pixies doing over there?' he said.

'Putting the hum into tops,' said the footman. 'But don't go too near. One of the hums might get into you by mistake, and that's *such* a nuisance, you know!'

They stood at a safe distance, watching. It was very interesting indeed. So many things were going on; there was so much to see and hear, that they almost forgot they were toys themselves.

'How's your growl, bear?' said a little pixie, running up to Moon-Face. He pressed him in the middle and Moon-Face growled deeply. 'Grrrrrr! Leave me alone! I don't like people doing that. Grrrrr!'

'Look – oh, look – isn't that Santa Claus himself?' cried Beth, suddenly, as a big man came into the room dressed in bright red. He wore a hood trimmed with white, and his jolly face had eyes that twinkled brightly.

'Yes. It's Santa Claus!' cried Joe. Santa Claus heard him and came over at once. He looked in surprise at Silky.

'Why!' he said, 'where did you come from? *You* weren't made in my castle, by pixies and goblins. You are the loveliest doll I've ever seen. I've a good mind to keep you for myself and put you at the very top of my own big Christmas Tree.'

'No, no, please not!' said Silky. Santa Claus looked down at the others. He seemed puzzled.

'Where do you all come from?' he said. 'I am quite sure I have never had any toys made like you. The rabbit, dressed up in kettles and saucepans, for instance – and this funny little bear. He doesn't seem like a proper teddy.'

'We're *not* proper toys!' said Beth. 'Santa Claus, we got turned into toys in the fort of the toy soldiers. I'm a little girl really.'

'And I'm Moon-Face, who lives at the top of the Faraway Tree,' said Moon-Face.

'What! The famous Moon-Face, who has a slippery-slip in his room, going down the tree from the top to the bottom!' cried Santa Claus. 'My goodness – I've often wanted to see that! Do you think I'm too fat to go down it?'

'No – no, I don't think so,' said Moon-Face, looking at him. 'I could give you *two* cushions to sit on instead of one. If you'd like to come now, you can go up and down the Faraway Tree as often as you like – we'll haul you up in the washing basket every time you arrive at the bottom, and you can slide down again from the top!'

'Let's go now,' said Santa Claus in delight. 'Well, well – to think I'm meeting the famous Moon-Face at last! And I suppose this lovely doll is Silky the fairy. And, of course – this is the Old Saucepan Man!'

'But – how do you know us?' asked Moon-Face, astonished.

'Oh, I've heard about you from the children,' said Santa Claus. 'They keep asking me for books about you, to go into their Christmas stockings and they looked so exciting that I read them all. I *did* want to meet you!'

Well, wasn't that a bit of luck? Santa Claus called his sleigh and they all got in. 'To the top of the Faraway Tree,' commanded Santa Claus, and away they went. It didn't take very long. In quite a little while the sleigh landed on a broad bough near the top of the tree, and they all got out.

'My room is just a bit higher up,' said Moon-Face,

and led the way. They were soon in his little round room. He pointed to the curious hole in the middle of the floor.

'There you are,' he said. 'That's the slippery-slip – it goes round and round from top to bottom of the tree – and you fly out of the trapdoor at the bottom, and land on a soft cushion of moss.'

'Splendid!' said Santa Claus. 'Will somebody else go first, please? Goodness, it's exactly the same as I read about in the books!'

'Er – do you think you could just change us back to our ordinary selves?' asked Joe, afraid that in his excitement Santa Claus might forget to do what they so badly wanted. 'I feel as if I'm going to somersault again, and I don't want to turn head-over-heels all the way down the slippery-slip.'

'Change you back? Yes, of course; it's easy!' said Santa Claus. 'The slippery-slip is just the right place for a spell. Shut your eyes, please.'

They all shut their eyes. Santa Claus touched each one gently, chanting a curious little song:

> 'Go in as you are,
> Come out as you were,
> Go in as you are,
> Come out as you were!'

They opened their eyes. Moon-Face got a cushion and

128

pulled Beth on to it. He gave her a tremendous push and she shot down the slippery-slip at top speed – round and round – and then out she flew through the trapdoor at the bottom, and landed on a tuft of moss.

'Oh,' she said, breathless. 'Oh! I'm myself again. I'm not a stiff-jointed doll any longer – and I can shut and open my eyes properly!'

She got up – and out of the trapdoor flew Joe. 'Joe! You're all right again! You're you!' cried Beth in delight. 'And here comes Silky – she's not a doll any more – and here's Frannie – she's all right, too. Look out – here's the Old Saucepan Man – yippee, he's back to normal!'

'And he's lost his floppy ears,' said Silky. 'I'm rather sorry. I liked him with those long ears. Good old Saucepan.'

And then, WhoooooOOOOOOSH! The trapdoor shot open with a bang and out sailed Santa Claus, his hood on the back of his head! Bump! He went on to the cushion of moss, and sat there, panting and full of delight.

'What a thrill! WHAT a thrill! Better than anything I've got in my castle.'

'Look out! Here comes Moon-Face!' cried Joe, and out came Moon-Face, no longer a fat teddy bear, but his own beaming self once more.

'I'd like to do that again,' said Santa Claus, standing up. 'How did you say we got back to the top of the tree?

129

In a basket?'

'Yes,' said Joe, 'but if you don't mind, we won't come with the others. You see, our mother will be wondering about us. So we'd better say goodbye and thank you very much.'

'Goodbye. See you next Christmas,' said Santa Claus. 'I'll bring you something extra nice. Ah – here comes the basket, let down on a rope. Do we get in?'

The last thing that Joe, Beth and Frannie saw was Santa Claus in the big basket, being pulled slowly up by all the squirrels at the top of the tree. Moon-Face and Silky and Saucepan were with him, leaning over the edge of the basket, waving to them.

'Well – I suppose dear old Santa Claus will be going down that slippery-slip till it's dark,' said Joe. 'Oh dear – surely I'm not going to turn head-over-heels again! I feel just like it!'

'Oh, you'll soon get out of the habit,' said Beth. 'I still feel as if I want to walk stiffly like a doll. Goodness, wasn't that an adventure!'

'We'll never have a better one,' said Frannie.

Oh yes, you will, Frannie, Beth and Joe. You just wait and see!

Enid Blyton

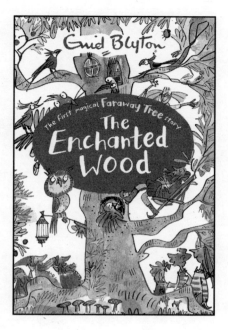

'*Up the Faraway Tree,*
Joe, Beth and me!'

Joe, Beth and Frannie move to the country and find an Enchanted Wood right on their doorstep! And in the wood stands the magic Faraway Tree where the Saucepan Man, Moon–Face and Silky the fairy live.

Together they visit the strange lands which lie at the top of the tree. They have the most exciting adventures – and plenty of narrow escapes!

Enid Blyton

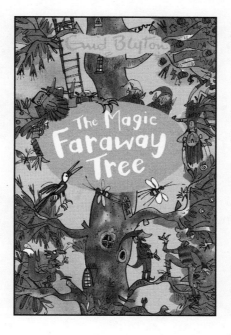

*'Oh, do let's take our lunch up into the
Land of Topsy-Turvy. Oh, do, do!'*

Rick thought it would be dull in the country with Joe,
Beth and Frannie. But that was before he found the
magic Faraway Tree!

They only have to climb through the cloud at
the top of the huge, magical tree to be in the Land
of Spells, or the Land of Topsy-Turvy, or even the Land
of Do-As-You-Please!

Enid Blyton

Joe, Beth and Frannie are fed up when they hear that Connie is coming to stay – she's so stuck-up and bossy. But that won't stop them from having exciting adventures with their friends Silky the fairy, Moon-Face and Saucepan Man.

Together they climb through the cloud at the top of the tree and visit all sorts of strange places, like the Land of Secrets and the Land of Treats – and Connie learns to behave herself!

EGMONT PRESS: ETHICAL PUBLISHING

Egmont Press is about turning writers into successful authors and children into passionate readers – producing books that enrich and entertain. As a responsible children's publisher, we go even further, considering the world in which our consumers are growing up.

Safety First
Naturally, all of our books meet legal safety requirements. But we go further than this; every book with play value is tested to the highest standards – if it fails, it's back to the drawing-board.

Made Fairly
We are working to ensure that the workers involved in our supply chain – the people that make our books – are treated with fairness and respect.

Responsible Forestry
We are committed to ensuring all our papers come from environmentally and socially responsible forest sources.

**For more information, please visit our website at
www.egmont.co.uk/ethical**